Think

by

C. G. Ferrel

Poems

ISBN 0-9729684-0-7

Library of Congress Control Number: 2003102706

To order a copy of this book, please visit your local bookstore. You may also order online at http://atlasbooks.com.

Quantity discounts are available on bulk purchases of this book for educational purposes, fundraising, etc. For details write to Acheulean Publishing, P.O. Box 6166, Rock Island, Illinois 61204. Please include phone number and name of contact person.

Reference Books

1. Personalities of America - Sixth Edition — Published by ABI (The American Biographical Institute).
2. International Directory of Distinguished Leadership - Fourth Edition — Published by ABI.
3. Who's Who in Poetry — Published by World of Poetry.
4. Who's Who in Poetry and Poet's Encyclopedia - Seventh Edition — Published by International Biographical Centre.

Publishing Credits - Poetry Anthologies
(contributor)

1. These Too Shall Be Heard Vol. I —Published by SA-DE Publications, Sam L. Vulgaris (Publisher), 1989.
2. These Too Shall Be Heard Vol. II —Published by SA-DE Publications, Sam L. Vulgaris (Publisher), 1989.
3. Golden Voices - Past and Present —Published by Fine Arts Press, Lincoln B. Young (Publisher), 1989.
4. 1990 Anthology of Southern Poetry —Published by Chuck Kramer, Great Lakes Poetry Press, Chuck Kramer (Publisher), 1990.
5. Whispers in the Wind Vol. III —Published by Quill Books, Shirley Mikkelson (Publisher), 1990.
6. American Poetry Anthology Vol. IX, No. 4 — Published by American Poetry Association, Robert Nelson (Publisher), 1990.
7. Down Peaceful Paths —Published by Quill Books, Shirley Mikkelson (Publisher), 1990.
8. Moments of Memories —Published by Publishers Press, 1990.
9. These Too Shall Be Heard Vol. III —Published by SA-DE Publications, Sam L. Vulgaris (Publisher), 1991.
10. American Poetry Anthology Vol. X, No. 2 — Published by American Poetry Association, Robert Nelson (Publisher), 1990.

11. Word Magic--A Panorama of Poetry —
Published by Fine Arts Press, Lincoln B. Young
(Publisher), 1991.
12. World of Poetry Anthology —Published by
World of Poetry Press, John Cambell (Editor &
Publisher), 1991.
13. Our World's Most Treasured Poems —
Published by World of Poetry Press, John
Cambell (Editor & Publisher), 1991.
14. Our World's Favorite Gold & Silver Poems —
Published by World of Poetry Press, John
Cambell (Editor & Publisher), 1991.
15. Poems That Will Last Forever —Published by
World of Poetry Press, John Cambell (Editor &
Publisher), 1991.
16. Great Poems of Our Time —Published by
World of Poetry Press, John Cambell (Editor &
Publisher), 1991.
17. Listen With Your Heart —Published by Quill
Books, 1992.
18. These Too Shall Be Heard, Vol. IV —Published
by SA-DE Publications
19. The Other Side of the Mirror —Published by
Watermark Press, 1992.
20. In A Different Light —Published by The
National Library of Poetry, 1992.
21. Our World's Most Favorite Poems —Published
by World of Poetry, 1991.
22. A Question of Balance —Published by The
National Library of Poetry, 1992.
23. Dance on the Horizon —Published by National
Library of Poetry
24. At Days End —National Library of Poetry

Biographical Data

Name: Carl G. Ferrel

Born: Iowa City, Iowa —July 29, 1950

Marital Status: Single

Education: Degree in Culinary Art - 1973; Studied Real Estate, Economics, Business Law and Communications - 1981, Black Hawk College.

Occupation(s): Chef, Meat Cutter, Business Consultant, President (record company), Restaurant Manager, Septic Surgeon. Also Real Estate Investor and Member of Laborers Union Local #309, Rock Island, Illinois.

Memberships have included:
- Florida State Poets Association, Inc.
- National Federation of State Poetry Societies, Inc.
- National Arbor Day Foundation
- Niabi Zoological Society
- National Parks & Conservation Association
- National & International Wildlife Federation
- World Wildlife Fund
- The National Audubon Society
- Associate Member of The American Museum of Natural History
- Associate Member of The Smithsonian Associates
- Associate Member of The Illinois Sheriffs' Association
- Associate Member of The Nature Conservancy

Awards:
- Golden Poet - 1990 & 1991
- Honorable Mentions (7)
- Distinguished Leadership - 1991
- Editors Choice Award - 1996

Statement (Common Themes and Comments): I write about a variety of subjects; love, friendship, family, nature, social issues, etc. I would like to see world peace, and an end to world hunger, and the formation of an international coalition to protect and preserve the earth and its inhabitants and strive for an ecological balance between man and nature that will allow both to survive and prosper. I would also like to see a return to traditional family values.

My Advice: Seek the truth in all things. Be honest, fair, and sincere.

For additional information see:
Bern Porter Collection of Contemporary Letters
Miller Library, Special Collections
Colby College
Waterville, Maine 04901

Table of Contents

WHY AM I HERE?

Why am I here,
I ask you, Mother dear?
To brighten my world,
My wonderful child.

Why am I here,
Father of mine?
To better this world,
When it is time.

Why am I here,
My very best friend?
To give support,
In troubled times.

Why am I here,
O Lord above?
To bring to the world,
Much needed love!

RING OF TRUTH

The ring of truth
Is all around.

You cannot see it
But it can be found!

GOING HOME

The night
Is bitter cold
As I huddle
Near the track.

Waiting
For the eastbound train,
To take me home
Again.

Back
To Illinois
And friends
I left behind.

Back
To my family
I have not seen
In years.

Ah! The Train
Is in my sights.
I am finally
Going home.

AVALANCHE

Boulders as big as cars
Ricocheted down the mountainside.

Trees were uprooted and
Added to the downward flow
Of debris.

Wildlife ran in search of shelter,
But there was none to be found.

Nothing; plant or animal,
Was safe from destruction.

Now there is silence,
In the valley below.

The anger,
Of the mountain,
Has silenced,
Life in the valley.

PRISONER

Cold sweat
Upon my brow.

Fear
In every bone.

Prison guards
Look away.

I won't
Be going home!

VISION OF THE DREAM

The dreamer sees a vision,
In the recess of his mind.

The architect puts on paper,
The outline of the dream.

The builder puts in concrete,
What the paper shows.

The world looks on in wonder,
At the vision of the dream.

SPRINGTIME IN WINTER

A breath of spring in winter
Came suddenly to me.

From the shadows of the past
She appeared one wintry day.

And for a fleeting moment,
The winter chill was gone.

And for a frozen moment,
My heart was warm again.

SEPARATE WAYS

With sadness
I am thinking
Of love
That is no more.

With passing time
We grew apart,
And went
Our separate ways.

Now memories
Are all I have,
Of love
That went away.

IN TOTAL SILENCE

In total silence waits
The man who is alone.

No family — no friends,
No future.

No
Words to speak,
No
One to hear.

The future mingles
With the past.

The present,
Remains the same!

THE LONGEST ROAD

The path of life
I have walked.
Through concrete jungles
I have stalked.

Yet what I hunt,
I do not know.
Still I search,
And on I go.

That path is long,
The Journey slow,
But as I travel
I learn and grow.

BLESSED IS THE MAN

Blessed is the man
That has the chance to stand,
Clinging gently to
His precious child's hand.

A wealthier man
Nowhere will be found.

The treasures of the world
Are the children of the land!

SHADOWS

Walking in the shadows
Of a brighter day.

With fondness I remember,
The triumphs of my youth.

The days when I
Were running free,
And full of boundless
Energy.

Those days I thought
Could never end.

But I am older now,
And wiser still.

Sad to say,
But, oh so true.

The truth
Is crystal clear.

Now, all that's left
Are memories
Of days
No longer here!

THE MIGHTY OAK

The old and twisted oak
In the forest bravely stands —
With gnarled fingers curled
And arms bent from age.

He towers like a giant
Over his sapling heirs —
Who wait in patient silence
For the chance to wear the crown.

But with his age is wisdom
And strength they've yet to know —
For now he will wear the stately crown
On his old and furrowed brow!

BILLY THE KID

William Bonney;
An outlaw,
Through and through.

He thought himself,
The fastest gun.
Until Pat Garret drew!

IT IS TIME

It is time;
To rise above the ashes,
Like a Phoenix to the sky.

To spread the words of wisdom,
To people near and far.

To right the wrongs of evil,
And let goodness rule the land.

It is time to work together,
To preserve this world so grand.

TEARDROP

The mind
Slowly wanders,
Of an old man
All alone.

Friends
Are but a memory
From a past
That is no more.

Evening
Brings a teardrop
To
An aging eye.

Morning
Brings a thought
Of a lady
In her youth.

And with it
Comes a smile
To an old
And wrinkled lip.

NO QUARTER GIVEN

I ask for no quarter,
And none do I give.

I only desire,
To live and let live!

LIVING WITH RELATIVES

I live in a state of limbo,
On eggshells carefully walk.

Words carefully chosen,
Insults taken in stride.

Pride that must be swallowed,
Feelings, hidden deep inside.

Afraid to be myself,
In front of company.

It is not easy to maintain,
A sense of humor all the time.

Living with relatives is hard,
But living alone is worse!

KIDS IN WINTER

The snow is falling very hard.

The kids are playing in the yard.

Throwing snowballs and having fun,
Playing cowboys and
Indians with little toy guns.

That's what kids in winter do.

That's how they also get the flu.

FAMILY

All the smiles,
All the tears,
All the laughter,
Throughout the years.

All the sorrow,
All the pain.
All the joy,
That love can bring.

THANKSGIVING DINNER

Women screaming everywhere,
Keep these kids out of our hair.

Biscuits baking in the oven,
Pies and cakes on the counter cooling.

Chicken and noodles in the pot,
Corn on the cob, nice and hot.

Potatoes, gravy, fresh baked ham,
Cranberries, sweet tasting yams.

Best of all — the turkey,
Oh, so juicy and golden brown.

Come on everybody, gather 'round,
Dinner is ready, it's time to sit down.

THE BEST OF TIMES

As I sit here rocking,
In my rocking chair,
Staring out my window,
At clouds that fill the air.

The rain comes gently pounding,
The fire leaps and crackles,
In my cozy fireplace.

Through it all I still remember,
When I was in my prime.

You were still here with me,
Those were the best of times!

LIGHT OF DAY

Dawn brings a twinkle,
To the eye of another day.

Birth brings a twinkle,
Much the same way.

A mother sees a child,
As the earth does see the light.

All things begin anew.

With no limit on the future,
Or places to explore.

All things are possible,
In the light of day.

FALLEN STAR

A maiden I saw,
Ever so far.

With beauty such,
I had to stare.

Long golden hair of silk,
Eyes of emerald green.

A lovelier woman,
I have seldom seen.

Sitting there,
In a smoke filled bar,
Reminding me,
Of a fallen star.

SHATTERED HEART

Bitter words -
The speeding bullet,
That shattered -
This heart of mine.

The universe -
The empty space,
Your going -
Left behind.

ONE TINY CANDLE

One tiny candle,
Burning in the night,
Removes me from darkness
And brings me to the light.

One tiny candle,
Keeps me safe within my room.
'Til the sun comes out tomorrow,
To chase away my gloom.

THE PRICE SUPREME

The day will come,
With payment due,
For all that drugs,
Have done to you.

Then, for the nightmare,
And the dream,
You must pay,
The price supreme!

ONCE, A PRETTY MAIDEN

Once, a pretty maiden,
Many years ago.
Now, a chubby house wife,
Four kids in a row.

Once, a handsome athlete,
Many years ago.
Now, a balding husband,
Four kids in a row.

Married life and middle age,
Help to set the stage,
For growing old,
And youth, so quickly lost.

ORANGE BLOSSOM

The scent of orange blossom,
Lingers in the air.

Though the wearer now,
Has long since left this room.

The vision of her beauty,
Forever will remain.

To shine like a beacon,
In an old and lonely heart.

PERCEPTION

Half empty was the cup,
Or was it perhaps half full.

A matter of perception,
Is all that can be said.

In sadness you may wish,
For things you do not have.

Or rejoice and be happy,
For things that you have.

The choice —
Is yours to make.

But just remember this my friend,
One life is all you have!

DRIFTER

I walk the lonely highway,
Dark and damp from recent rain.

I have no special destiny,
No place to call my home.

From town to town I wander.

Always I am the stranger,
To everyone I pass.

Destined to be a drifter,
Until I breathe my last!

TODAY, TOMORROW & YESTERDAY

Yesterday;
Forever gone.

Tomorrow;
Never comes.

Today;
Always here!

A LIE IS A LIE

A truth
Veiled in falsehood,
Is not
A truth at all!

COMES THE DAWN

Slowly set the sun,
That ends the light of day.

Silent;
Comes the night.

Allowing evil,
Then to lurk.

Just as surely,
Comes the dawn.

Defeating darkness,
Once again.

LIGHT OF JESUS

The light of Jesus brightly shines,
To guide; and constantly remind us.

Of all the reasons that he died,
And things that we should live for.

Peace; Truth; Justice,
And Freedom — for all mankind!

THE SIMPLE THINGS THAT COUNT

A crying child
In my arms.

Around my neck,
A good luck charm.

In the other room,
A loving wife.

What more can I say,
It's a beautiful life.

Our life is simple
But very good.

We always have
Ample food.

A good roof
Over our heads.

Good clothing,
Cozy beds.

We are folks
Of little means.

But we are folks
Of simple needs!

A DAY OF REST

A day of rest and repose
Is a day to relax, I suppose.

Yet there never seems to be
A day of rest, just for me.

If it isn't one thing, it's another,
If it isn't my sister, it's my brother.

Someday I'm sure, there will be
A day of rest, just for me.

For if I have to, I'll go far away,
And until I'm rested, there I'll stay.

Only coming back, you see,
When I've had that day of rest, just for me!

STANDING IN THE SHADOWS

Standing in the shadow,
I see a lonely man.

He does not seem to fit,
No matter where he stands.

He tries to step into the light,
And blend in with the crowd.

He tries to be as others are,
But to no avail.

Out of time, out of place,
Somehow, he still remains,
Standing on the side lines,
Left out of the game.

THE ROSE

Bathed in gentle rain,
Nourished by the sun.

Protected by the thorn,
Enjoyed by everyone!

VOLCANO

Fire rising,
To the heaven,
Sending ash,
To darken sky.

Fleeing creatures,
Run for safety,
In the valley,
Far below.

The mountain shudders,
The forest burns.

But after midnight,
Life returns.

COMET

A ball of fire,
A flash of light,
Speeding swiftly,
Through the night.

Streaking through the starlit sky,
Destiny unknown.

It came from out of nowhere,
And to nowhere quickly went.

Now the sky is back to normal,
And only stars light up the night.

ANOTHER BROKEN HEART

Another heart is broken,
Another love has died.

Another lonely soul,
Has been cast aside!

PRIDE

You may keep me poor,
You may keep me hungry,
But my pride will always be!

You may take away my freedom,
You may bind me up in chains,
But my pride will always be!

You may put me in a cage,
And try to still my rage,
But my pride will always be!

You may ridicule and scorn me,
You may torture and abuse me,
But my pride will always be!

You may stab or even shoot me,
But until you finally kill me,
My pride will always be!

THE FUTURE OF HUMANITY

The future of humanity
In the child's hand does rest.

For the future of our children,
We must do our best,
To protect and preserve
The only world we have.

For we are the caretakers
Of the world in which we live.

RAINBOW

Red, yellow, orange, green
The rainbow — after a summer rain.

The air — crisp, cool, clean
All things, are new again.

ALONE UNTO MYSELF

Alone unto myself,
I sit and meditate.

Reflecting
On the past,
Calling forth
Old memories,
Buried deep
Within my soul.

Of glory days,
Forgotten youth,
And time,
Forever gone!

IF I CLOSE MY EYES

If I close my eyes,
I cannot see the pain.

If I close my ears,
I cannot hear the cries.

If I close my heart,
I will not feel the joy.

If I close my mind,
I will not learn to live!

ISOLATION

Compelled to live in silence,
Not allowed to speak.

Alone in isolation,
Days turn into weeks.

Total
Is the darkness,
My only company.

Somewhere
Must be a candle
In the shadow
Of the soul.

To light
The way to freedom,
Where
I finally can be heard!

LOVE VS. WAR

Love;
The Beginning.
Adam and Eve.

War;
The End.
Atom Bomb,
Eve of Destruction!

TO HELP ME THINK

I went to town
To get a drink,
Meant perhaps
To help me think.

Many thinkers
Go to town.
But in a bottle,
Most do drown!

THE PAIN OF LONELINESS

Alone
In a crowded room.
In silence
Among the roar.

Faced
With endless gloom.
He
Can take no more.

The pain
Inside his head,
Will never
Go away.

It remains
With him instead,
Until
His dying day!

NO ESCAPE

I run
And run, to
Get away.

Yet,
My past
Seems closer
Every day!

PENDULUM

The pendulum
Swings to the right,
And an old man
Dies alone.

The pendulum
Swings to the left,
And a baby boy
Is born.

The books of nature
Balanced
With life and death
Each day!

FINAL THOUGHT

As I walk
My six by eight,
I think about
"The Pearly Gate."

I think of heaven
And of hell.

I lay on my bunk,
Thinking, well,
Maybe I'll make it,
Maybe I won't.

But I'll burn in hell,
If I don't!

MINDS EYE

My minds eye
Sees crystal clear,
The job
That must be done.

Feed the hungry,
House the homeless,
Bring peace
To everyone.

Make this world
A better place,
For generations,
Yet to come!

CHRISTMAS TIME

A blanket,
Made of white.
A tree
Of piney green.

A rainbow
Of colored lights
To decorate
The tree.

A house
Full of children.
With faces
Smiling bright.

A ham
Baked to perfection.
A turkey,
Golden brown.

And most of all,
Old Santa.
Who, every year
Comes 'round!

A NEW YEAR

The year 2000
Is no more.
2001,
Is at the door.

Every day is special,
Every friend
Is dear.

Care
For those you love
And have
A Happy New Year!

MERRY CHRISTMAS

Christmas time
Is finally here.
A joyous time
At end of year.

All
The best,
I wish
For you.

Good health,
Good cheer.
All throughout
The coming year!

VALENTINE'S DAY

Such
A special person,
Deserves
A special day.

Today,
I give you chocolate.
Because
You are so sweet.

Today,
I give a rose to you.
Because
You are so beautiful.

Today,
I give a card to you.
To say how very special,
You always are to me.

You also get my heart.
To show
How blessed I feel,
For every day with you!

WHISKEY BOTTLE

Whiskey bottle
On the shelf
Oh,
How I adore thee.

The way
You warm me up
Down
Deep inside.

The way you
Comfort
And
Amuse me.

Though there are
Those other times
When you deceive
And confuse me.

Yet, somehow
I always know
You will be there,
When I need you!

ABE LINCOLN

Tall and slender was he,
This man from Illinois.

A man of the land,
And a lawyer as well,
This man from Illinois.

Sincere of heart,
Eloquent of speech,
This man from Illinois.

He was our sixteenth
President.
This man from Illinois.

With passion he delivered,
His "Gettsyburg Address."
And stirred the hearts
Of man and boy,
This man from Illinois.

MANBEAST

The laughter
Roars like thunder.
When life
And times are good.

But
When life is hard
And
Times are bad,
The heart
Fills with sadness,
And teardrops
Freely flow.
For such
Is the nature
Of he
That is the manbeast.

He weeps
In times of famine.
And rejoices
When he can feast!

ICE MISTRESS

If you love only money,
Your mistress
Will be cold.

She will not
Make you happy,
Or prevent
Growing old.

And when
Your time does come,
You
Will die alone!

FINAL TRUTH

When you sit
In silence,
In the light
Of final truth.

Then you
Shall have the answers,
To the questions
Of your youth!

TIDES OF CHANGE

The tides of change
Swiftly rushes by.

The future
Soon becomes the past.

The world
As we know it,
We know
Can never last.

FREEDOM OF SPEECH

You may
Take away my job
And make me
A beggar man.

You can
Take away my legs
So I can
No longer stand.

But, as long
As I can breathe
And have a voice
With which to speak.

You cannot
Still my words,
Or alter
Where they reach!

INNER THOUGHTS

One day
While I was walking,
With myself
I did some talking.

About the future
Of humanity,
And the part
That I must play.

To make this world
A better place,
For
Future generations.

AVERAGE WORKING MAN

From the break of day
Until the sun has set,
I toil long and hard,
As the sweat beads my brow.

I do my job in earnest,
Take pride in work well done.

Just an average working man,
Most folks would surely say.

If average work is what I do,
And average that I am.

Then average I would like to stay,
Doing the best I can.

VALLEY OF THE SUN

In the valley
Of the sun,
Where time,
Stands forever still.

An ancient culture
Does survive.
Preserved
By people proud.

Who keep alive
Traditions,
From
Their distant past.

And live the way
They have always done,
In the valley
Of the sun!

THE SKY, THE EARTH
AND ONE TRUE LOVE

The sky is filled
With mystery.
The earth is abundant
With places to see.

I cannot travel
Through outer space.
So I will do my searching in an earthly place.

Hunting places
To explore
Gathering things
I much adore.

But though I travel
Far and wide,
My love for her
Will abide!

NO SECOND THOUGHT

We are the method
Of our own demise.
We kill and destroy
Never thinking twice.

We rob the land
Of precious treasure.
We take and take
And never give.

We kill
So many creatures
That want
So much to live!

THE ONLY CONSTANT

The only constant
Is constant change.
Control by man,
Is near an end.

The earth can take
Little more
Of modern man,
Breaking nature's laws!

THE COMING STORM

A howling wind
Outside my door.
Evidence;
A storm is near.

Coming closer.
Closer still.
Impressing all
With iron will.

Hell bent
On destruction
Of everything
In it's path.

All things
Are affected,
By
The coming storm.

SEASONS SWIFTLY PASS

Seasons
Pass so swiftly.
And youth
So quickly gone.

One day, running,
Laughing, playing.
The next, rocking
And remembering!

WHAT EVER IT'S WORTH

He who walks
In the darkest night,
Is the one who battles
In the toughest fight.

He does not know
If he will win.
He does not care
If he must sin.

As long as he
Does not perish,
From this life
He does so cherish!

TARNISHED REPUTATION

Though I was judged
Most innocent,
And the law
Did set me free.

Still I,
With
Tarnished reputation
Be!

COOL YOURSELF

I look
Upon the water.
My reflection
Beckons me.

Come take a dip,
Cool yourself,
Is what
It says to me!

THE NIGHT

You may walk
Or you may run.
You may hide out
From the sun.

But in the dark
Or in the light,
You cannot escape
From the night!

THERE IS ALWAYS TOMORROW

A life of solitude
Is a life forsook.
Sometimes I wish
My life were took.

I look in the mirror
Only to see,
A hollow existence,
Staring back at me.

But then
I always smile some.
For I know
The day will come.

When
I will see the rise
Of
An illustrious sun!

ALL THAT IS ACCEPTED

All
That is accepted
Is
Not always right.

Change
May be required
So
We can see the light!

THE DANCING LIGHT

At the break of day,
He emerges from his cold and lonely cave.

To seek the warmth of daylight,
To ease the chill within his bones.

And there, not far away,
A brightness on the ground.

With caution he approached,
To explore this mystery.

And much to his surprise,
This dancing light gave off a glow,
That warmed his very soul.

The light he soon discovered,
Was attached to a fallen tree.

An idea quickly formed,
In the recess of his mind.

With a smaller branch
That he could carry,
He would steal
The dancing light.

And take it to his cave,
To keep him warm at night.

STRANGER

Everywhere I go,
I seem so out of place.
Everywhere I go,
I wear a stranger's face.

It seems as though,
Here I don't belong.
And everywhere I go,
Everything I do is wrong.

I drift through the day,
I stumble through the night.
No matter what I do,
It never does seem right.

Is there a place?
Is there a time?
When things for once,
Will turn out fine.

To this, the answer,
I do not know.
Yet, on the path of life,
I continue to go.

I have searched here,
I have searched there,
I have searched
Most everywhere.

Still, answers to my questions,
I have not found.
So I continue to search,
And keep my feet upon the ground.

LAST DRINK

He staggered as he walked,
So full of rum was he.

He bellied up to the bar,
To order once again.

He mumbled words
That were not clear,
And slobbered,
On his shirt.

The barmaid asked him,
To repeat,
The words,
That he had said.

But all he did
Was stare at her,
With bloodshot eyes a-bulging,
From the sockets in his head.

He took a breath — closed his eyes,
Fell crashing to the floor.

Now he would drink, never more,
Alas, the drunk was dead!

MOTHER'S DAY

A flower
For your mother,
Any kind will do.

A card, with just a word, or two.

To remind her
That you love her,
The way
That she loves you.

Not so much to ask,
Just one time each year.

When everyday,
While growing up,
She was always there!

THE LAST TOMORROW

When the last river is poisoned
And the last fish has died,
It will be the last tomorrow.
But will you wonder why?

When the air is not fit to breathe
And the last bird leaves the sky,
It will be the last tomorrow.
But will you wonder why?

When the last tree is felled
And the forest is no more,
It will be the last tomorrow.
But will you wonder why?

When the earth has turned to desert
And the last flower wilts,
It will be the last tomorrow.
But will you wonder why?

When the last bomb is dropped
And the last baby cries,
It will be the last tomorrow.
But will you wonder why?